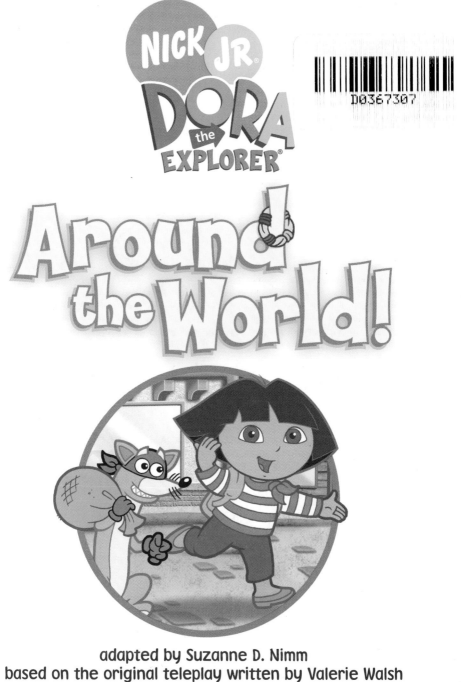

NICK JR.
DORA the EXPLORER®

Around the World!

adapted by Suzanne D. Nimm
based on the original teleplay written by Valerie Walsh
illustrated by Ron Zalme

Ready-to-Read

Simon Spotlight/Nick Jr.
New York   London   Toronto   Sydney

Based on the TV series *Dora the Explorer*® as seen on Nick Jr.®

SIMON SPOTLIGHT
An imprint of Simon & Schuster Children's Publishing Division
1230 Avenue of the Americas, New York, New York 10020
© 2006 Viacom International Inc. All rights reserved.
NICK JR., *Dora the Explorer,* and all related titles, logos, and characters
are registered trademarks of Viacom International Inc.
All rights reserved, including the right of reproduction in whole or in part in any form.
SIMON SPOTLIGHT, READY-TO-READ, and colophon
are registered trademarks of Simon & Schuster, Inc.
Manufactured in the United States of America
2 4 6 8 10 9 7 5 3
Library of Congress Cataloging-in-Publication Data
Nimm, Suzanne D.
Around the world! / adapted by Suzanne D. Nimm; based on the original teleplay written by
Valerie Walsh; illustrated by Ron Zalme.—1st ed.
p. cm.—(Dora the explorer) (Ready-to-read)
"Based on the TV series Dora the Explorer as seen on Nick Jr."—T.p. verso.
ISBN-13: 978-1-4169-2478-4
ISBN-10: 1-4169-2478-7
I. Zalme, Ron. II. Dora the explorer (Television program) III. Title.
PZ7.N5896Ar 2006
2006016343

Hi! I am .

Today is Friendship Day!

SWIPER

swiped all

of the friendship BRACELETS !

Now we have to return them

to our friends around the WORLD !

Will you help us

deliver the friendship  ?

BRACELETS

Great!

MAP says that we

have to bring 🔗 **BRACELETS**

to our friends

at the 🗼 **TOWER** in France,

the  in Tanzania,
MOUNTAIN

the ⌂ in Russia,
PALACE

and the Great ▨ of China.
WALL

We are in France!

Where is the Eiffel ?

TOWER

We have to follow the road with 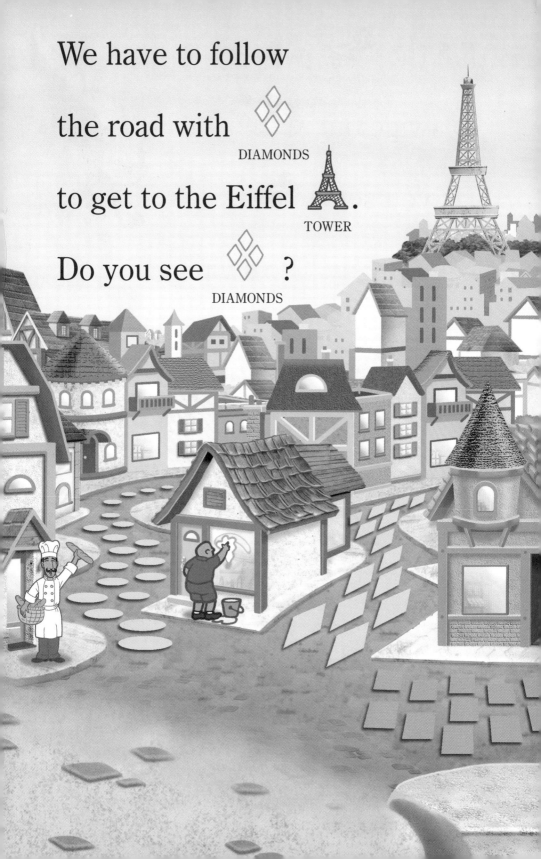 **DIAMONDS** to get to the Eiffel **TOWER**. Do you see **DIAMONDS**?

Fifi the will try

SKUNK

to swipe our !

BRACELETS

Do you see a ?

SKUNK

Oh, no! Say "No swiping!"

Thanks for stopping the !

SKUNK

Now our friends in France

can get friendship .

BRACELETS

We are in Tanzania!

This  is giving us
ELEPHANT

a ride to the .
MOUNTAIN

Look! I see a  and a .
ZEBRA   LION

Uh-oh! Sami the  will try
HYENA

to swipe the friendship .
BRACELETS

If you see a , say
HYENA

"No swiping!"

All of our friends

are so happy

to get their  !

BRACELETS

Next we have to ride in a 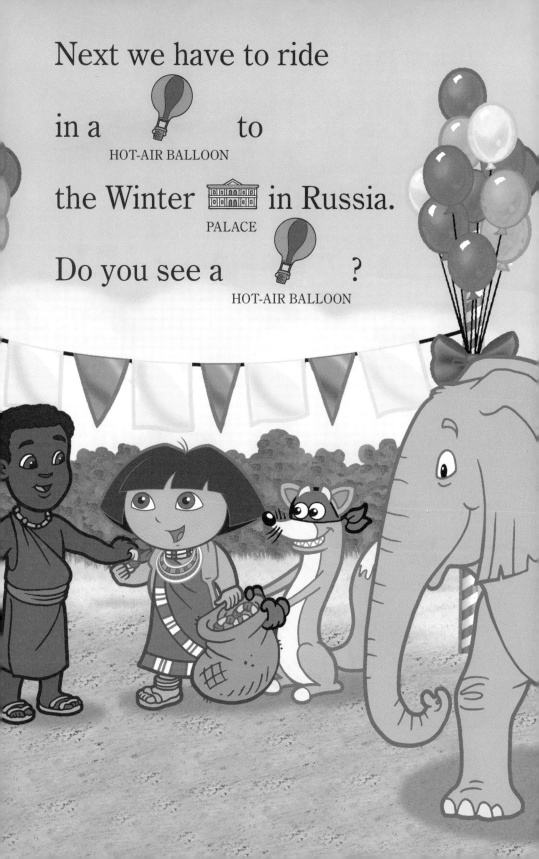 to the Winter PALACE in Russia.

HOT-AIR BALLOON

Do you see a 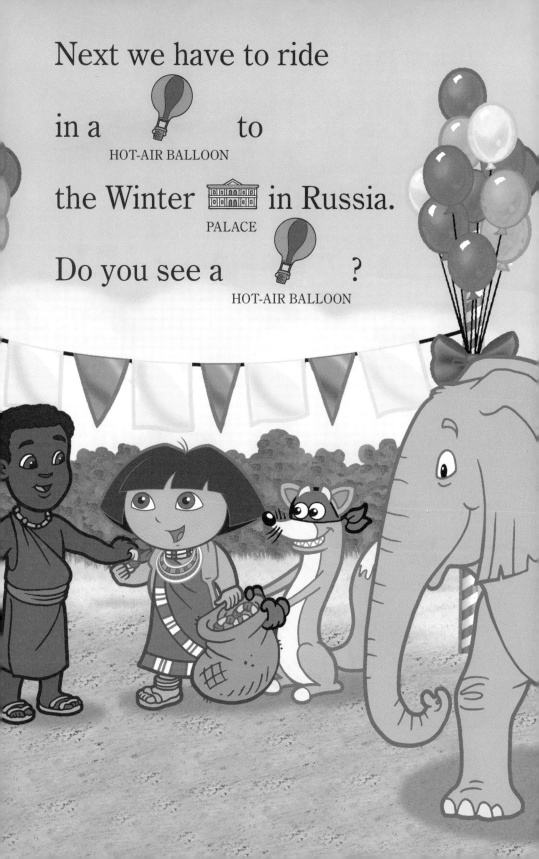 ?

HOT-AIR BALLOON

It is a cold and snowy day.

has just

what we need!

BACKPACK

Do you see a  COAT , MITTENS ,

a HAT , and SKIS ?

Now we can give out

friendship  BRACELETS

to our friends in Russia.

Look! One  is different
SNOWMAN

from the other  .
SNOWMAN

Wait—it is Fomkah the

sneaky !

BEAR

Fomkah wants to swipe

the friendship .

BRACELETS

Say "No swiping!"

Now we can give out

the  to our friends
BRACELETS

at the Great of China.
WALL

Ying-Ying the 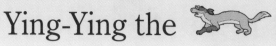 WEASEL

will try to swipe the BRACELETS.

Say "No swiping!"

Look! There is one  left.

BRACELET

It is a friendship  for !
BRACELET   SWIPER

Now everyone has a  .
BRACELET

Thank you for helping us

deliver the friendship

BRACELETS

to all our friends around the 🌍 !

WORLD

Happy Friendship Day!